Lalaloopsy
Sew Magical! Sew Cute!

Let's Grow a Garden!

by Lauren Cecil

New York   Toronto   London   Mexico City   New Delhi   Hong Kong

ISBN 978-0-545-39218-1

12 11 10 9 8 7 6 5 4 3 2 1

12 13 14 15 16 / 0

Designed by Angela Jun
Printed in the U.S.A.
First printing, January 2012

40

It was nearly springtime. Blossom Flowerpot and Spot Splatter Splash were taking a stroll through the park.

"I love the park in springtime," Spot said. "But I feel like something is missing. . . ."

"I know what it is," Blossom replied. "Flowers!"

"That's it! Some colorful flowers are just what this park needs!" Spot agreed.

"Spring is the perfect time to plant a garden with lots of colorful things in it," Blossom said. "What are we waiting for?"

Spot and Blossom rushed to Bea Spells-a-Lot's house. "We're going to plant a garden!" Blossom said. "Do you have any books that could help?"

"I have just the thing," Bea said.

"Thanks!" Spot said.

Blossom and Spot looked for a perfect place for their garden. "This is big enough to plant flowers and vegetables," Blossom said. "But it'll take a lot of work."

"Let's see if our friends want to help," Spot suggested. "It'll be more fun if we work together."

The next day, all the Lalaloopsy girls came to help plant the garden.

"I'm so glad you are here!" Blossom said. "We're going to have a great time."

"**B**ut we've never planted a garden before," Mittens Fluff 'n' Stuff said. "How will we know what to do?"

"Don't worry. I'll show you everything you need to know," Blossom said.

"First we have to pull out the weeds," Blossom explained.
"But won't I get dirty?" Jewel Sparkles asked.
"Sometimes it's fun to get a little dirty," Blossom said. Then she yanked out a weed. "Dig in!"

"**N**ext we need to turn over the soil," Blossom said.

"Phew!" Pillow Featherbed sighed. "This is making me tired!"

"Gardening's hard work," Blossom said. "It's okay if you need to take a little break."

"Now it's time to plant the seeds," Blossom said.

"Let's plant some night-blooming moonflowers," Dot Starlight suggested. "They're my favorite!"

"Great idea!" Blossom agreed.

"We need to give the seeds lots of water," Blossom explained. "They're very thirsty."

"So am I!" Mittens said. "All this work is making me hot."

"Have some water," Blossom said. "It will cool you off."

"There! All the seeds are planted," Blossom said. "Now we just have to wait."

"When will the vegetables be ready?" Crumbs Sugar Cookie asked.

"It takes plants a little while to grow," Blossom said. "We have to be patient."

The Lalaloopsy girls returned to the garden several days later. Little sprouts were peeking from the dirt.
"Our seeds have sprouted!" Blossom cried.

"I thought they'd be bigger," Dot said. "What's taking so long?"
"Sprouts are baby plants," Blossom explained. "It takes them time to become grown-ups. We'll come back again soon."

When the Lalaloopsy girls came back, the garden looked very different. The flowers were blooming and the veggies were plump and ripe.

"Wow! Look how big everything is!" Jewel said.

"The best part is yet to come," Blossom replied.

"What's that?" Pillow asked.

"Time to pick everything," Blossom said. "Let's get to work!"

The girls picked all the vegetables and flowers that they'd grown. Their garden had turned out great!

"What are we going to do with all these vegetables?" Spot asked.
"I have an idea!" Crumbs said. "Let's have a picnic! I'll make carrot muffins."

"Great idea!" Blossom said.

The girls prepared a great big meal with all the vegetables. And they made beautiful bouquets with the flowers.

"*Mmmm!*" Peanut Big Top said as she crunched into a carrot. "Everything tastes so fresh!"

"Vegetables always taste better when you've grown them yourself," Blossom said.

"So, did you enjoy planting a garden?" Blossom asked.

"It was a lot of hard work," Pillow said.

"But it was worth it," Jewel added, "especially since we got to spend time with our friends."